Kitten

Steel Security Prequel

Charity Parkerson

Punk & Sissy Publications

Copyright

—Warning: This book is intended for readers over the age of 18. Some of my books contain allusions to past abuse and trauma.

CONTENTS

Introduction

All Clover wants for Christmas is a job. He never expects Saint Knack, or that all Saint wants this holiday is him.

When Clover started working at sixteen, he loved his job with all his heart. He hoped to stay there forever. However, when they hire his ex to be his manager, Clover is out. Unfortunately, he never thought it would be so hard to get work this time of year. When he spots the ad for an office manager for a personal security company, he doesn't think he has much of a chance. That is, until he meets Saint.

When Clover walks into Saint's office, Saint is more than a little shocked by the tall, skinny kitten in front of him. Seriously, he's dressed like a kitten. After five minutes in Clover's company, not only is Saint certain Clover is perfect for the job, he's even more certain he's also exactly what Saint needs for himself.

Kitten is a whirlwind, insta-love holiday story giving a peek into Charity Parkerson's series: Steel Security. This series deals with some of the toughest bodyguards in the country falling hard for men they never see coming.

Author Note

THIS ONE INCLUDES A past abusive relationship.

CHAPTER ONE

THERE WAS NOTHING BUT a glass door that read: Steel Security. In smaller letters underneath, it was dubbed location three. The bland door was part of a business strip right off the Square in small town Washington. The state, not DC. Clover always had random nonsensical thoughts when he was nervous, and he was anxious as hell. Part of Clover had always hoped he could stay at his first and only job forever. Then that ridiculous Jacobe had ratcheted up his stalking efforts by getting hired as his manager. Clover had quit on the spot with no plan. He had applied to dozens of jobs as soon as he got home. So far, Steel Security had been the first to call. Funnily enough, it was the one he had been certain wouldn't be interested in him.

Taking a deep breath, he pulled off his knit cap and gloves. Clover squared his shoulders and walked inside like he owned the place. A bell jingled above the door. At least he could pretend it was a Christmas decoration. The wind sort of went out of sails when he found nothing but a front office area. He smelled coffee, but he didn't see anyone. There was also nothing decorated to celebrate the season. Every other business, all around and on the square, was brightly decked out.

The lack of Christmas cheer gave him a bad feeling about the man in charge's temperament. Then a massive bear of a man stepped out from a side office. He was all smiles and appeared genuinely fun loving.

"Hey. You must be Clover."

Clover nodded. He moved forward with his hand extended for Mr. Knack to shake. "That's me. You must be Mr. Knack."

His—hopefully—new boss smiled even brighter. If Clover wasn't desperately poor, and scared as hell he wouldn't land this job, he would flirt his ass off heavily right now. He loved a bear. Most of the time, they were straight, unfortunately. That was very likely the case for Saint Knack. His laughter-filled blue eyes and gorgeous dark hair made him damn near sigh worthy.

"It's just Saint. Come in. Have a seat."

He shuffled inside the office, following on Saint's heels. His gaze automatically dropped to Saint's ass. Damn. That was how someone filled a pair of jeans. Now was not the time for his hormones to take control.

Before Clover said a word to save himself from this untimely longing, Saint glanced over his shoulder, nearly catching Clover ogling him. "You have an impressive resume. Ten years at the same job these days. You must be very loyal." He sat behind his desk and focused on Clover.

Clover sat on the edge of the chair across from Saint and clasped his hands between his knees. A shiver ran through him. He had been so nervous, he hadn't realized how cold it was.

At his reaction, Saint winced. "Yeah. Sorry about the cold. The heat is out. I've called for a repairman, but he can't come until late this afternoon."

As much as Clover hated being cold, he put on a brave face. "I'm not surprised. The weather has been especially brutal. I've lived here my entire life, and I can't recall it ever being this bad. It's probably taxing units all over town, keeping the repairmen hopping."

Saint nodded. "You can't tell me climate change isn't real."

Oh. He liked Saint. "Exactly!"

They shared a smile.

Saint dropped his gaze to what was obviously Clover's resume. It looked as if he had scribbled several notes on it. That wasn't terrifying at all. Of course, the next thing out of Saint's mouth was the one thing Clover least wanted to answer.

"It looks like your last job was your only one. Why did you decide to leave?"

Clover tried to skirt the inquiry. "I loved working there. The last thing I wanted was to leave."

Saint's eyebrows rose. "But?"

Clover took a deep breath. Saint looked too nice. He couldn't stop himself. "Well, truthfully, about eight months ago, I caught my fiancé in bed with someone else. When I broke things off, he went completely ballistic, as if I was at fault. He started stalking me everywhere I went.

9

Last week, my former employer hired him to be my manager."

"Geez. It sounds like you need our services every bit as much as you need a job." His expression changed, turning fierce. "I want a full description, name, make and model of his car. Anything and as much as you can tell me. He won't be getting anywhere near this office. You'll definitely be safe at work."

It sounded like he had the job. Clover was scared to hope.

"Let's go."

Clover stood at Saint's demand. He followed Saint back into the front office area.

Saint motioned toward the chair behind the desk. Clover sat. Saint pointed at the telephone in front of Clover. "It looks like you did a lot of answering phones at your last job. That'll be the biggest part of your role here. Eventually, I'd love to train you to assign the guys to clients, ensuring no one is double-booked. That's a computer program I'll have to walk you through, but not today. When you answer—"

"Excuse me," Clover said, interrupting. "This sounds a lot like the position is mine."

Another heart-stopping smile snapped to Saint's lips. "Yeah. The job is around fifteen thousand more a year than your last position. We also offer health, dental, vision and 401K benefits, which we match. Does that work for you?"

Clover tried not to squeal. More money. Benefits. That sounded like a dream.

"That's perfect." Damn. Clover sounded too chipper, even to him.

Saint gave him a sharp nod. "Now, back to the phone. Do you need me to walk through how to transfer calls?"

Clover eyed the system. "Nope. This is the same system as my last job."

"Good boy."

Oh God. He wanted to hear that against his skin.

Saint kept talking as if he always spoke to everyone like that. "When you answer, don't do any sort of 'How may I help you?' Just say something like, 'Good morning. Steel Security.' You can come up with whatever you're comfortable with. But if you try to ask people how you can help them, they'll jump right in and tell you everything, expecting you'll know what to actually do."

Clover chuckled. He appreciated that. "I know exactly what you mean. At my last job, I was expected to ask people how I could help them. Considering it was a medical practice, the things I heard before I told them I was only the receptionist." Clover gave a dramatic shiver, except the shaking was kind of real. It had to be every bit of only thirty degrees in the office.

Another bright smile met his words. Saint pointed at a specific line: line three. "That's my office." He motioned toward his open office door. "If you need me, or all else fails, just shout my name. If you're good, I'll leave you to it." He turned away and immediately spun right back around. "Oh. Lunch is twelve to one. Instructions are taped to the desk, listing how to trans-fer calls to our answering service. Also, I don't care if you're on your cellphone or laptop or whatever, as long as your job is getting done."

Clover nodded. At least he wouldn't sit around bored. "Thank you for giving me a shot."

Saint winked. "I should be thanking you. I've been drowning around here alone."

Clover felt how bright his smile was. That wink alone had warmed the place by twenty degrees. He waited until Saint dis-appeared inside his office to relax. First things first. Clover donned his hat and pulled his gloves back on. He wished he had an electric blanket or something. With nothing left to do, Clover made that list of Jacobe's information. If nothing else, maybe he would get a few hours' peace during the day.

Saint dove into work, trying not to think too much about the cold, or the gorgeous man sitting up front. He had not been prepared. Saint had guessed the Asian descent by his last name: Clover Zhao. But Saint hadn't been ready in the least for the bright magenta hair, full face of perfectly done makeup, and pink outfit. He was beautiful. For a second, when he had seen Clover's approach on the security monitor, he had thought Clover might have been a woman. Then Clover had stepped inside, and Saint's mind melted. Wow, though. He was stunning. Saint had made dozens of notes on Clover's resume. Then Clover sat across from him and Saint lost his ability to focus. Saint would have to be careful. As much as he was a fighter, he was also a lover. He could easily cross the line. The last thing he needed was to end up sued. Steel would not appreciate that.

The familiar sound of a ringing phone had Saint on his feet. He was so used to manning both desks, Saint was trained like a dog to jump at the sound of a ringing phone. Even when he realized he didn't have to do that any longer, he still found his feet moving, gravitating toward Clover. A smile exploded across his face. Clover wore kitty paw gloves and a stocking cap that looked like cat ears. Fuck. He was adorable. Saint sat on Clover's desk and openly eavesdropped.

Clover flashed him a smile while obviously waiting for the person on the other end of the line to stop talking. Then he gasped. He set his hand on Saint's arm, as if asking him not to run away. Even through his gloves, Saint felt how Clover's fingers were ice. "*No*. Scandal. My boss—"

His caller obviously cut him off again.

Saint held up one finger and jogged to the storage closet. He found an old space heater they rarely used. Saint hoped it still worked. It was small, but it blew out some warm air. Saint wasn't trying to freeze the guy. That might end in a different lawsuit. But Saint knew the real reason he needed Clover comfortable. The guy was definitely worthy of the princess treatment.

With heater in hand, he jogged back to Clover's desk. It looked as if he was still trapped. Saint quickly plugged in the heater and got it going. It took it a second to actually blow out warm air and the smell of burning dust was strong. Still, he tugged his kitten's frozen paw toward the heat, holding it there. The pure look of orgasmic pleasure that settled on Clover's features made Saint's mouth dry. Saint couldn't look away. He was so transfixed, when Clover spoke, it startled Saint.

"That sounds horrific. Anything could've happened to you. My boss, Saint, is sitting right here. If anyone can make this right, it's him. I'll transfer you. But please call me later and tell me how you are. I'm terrified on your behalf."

Fuck. He was wonderful.

Clover motioned toward Saint's office. Taking the hint, Saint quickly returned to his desk. The phone on his desk rang.

Saint answered, "This is Saint."

"Hey, Saint. It's Maya Heartland. I'm pretty sure you're who I signed my contract with."

Oh no. It was one of their biggest clients. "I am. Is everything okay?"

She blew out a loud breath. "First off, whoever answers your phone is top tier. You should've sent him to me."

Saint covered his eyes. Fucking Leon. He should have fired that guy a long time ago. Saint had hoped pairing him with such a huge celebrity would make him proud and he would work harder. He tried to infuse some humor into his tone. "As much as Clover is a treasure, I'm not sure that's who you want protecting you. Unless you're looking for a six-foot twink in full makeup." He wouldn't have risked the quip if Maya wasn't such an advocate for the gay community. Saint had hoped to calm her.

"I'd take that any day over who you've sent." The rage in her voice couldn't be missed. Saint snapped his lips together and listened. "We were on our way to the set and I decided to stop to check out a tiny vintage shop along the way. At first, Leon did what I expected. He made sure the shop was empty and then guarded the door to ensure no one came in while I quickly looked at what they carry. Except when I stepped outside again, he was gone. Literally nowhere in sight. By three steps out the door, I was absolutely mobbed. Even the cute lamp I'd bought was knocked from my hand and shattered on the sidewalk. I had to fight my way back to the car. Thankfully, my driver jumped out and protected me until I was safe, and she's a woman who probably isn't a hundred pounds soaking wet. So, yes, I would be infinitely better protected with Clover."

Saint pinched the spot between his eyes. Clover was right. Maya could have been killed. Then what? Not only would the world have lost one of the sweetest actresses to grace the big screen, but Steel Security would be done for. Their reputation would be in ruins after losing a second client. Granted, that had been several years back. Most people probably didn't recall they were the security team who didn't protect Jayda when it mattered.

Saint dropped his hand. "I'm beyond horrified and sorry this happened. Is Leon still around?"

"No. We decided to leave, my driver and I, for safety's sake. I have no clue where he is. But he knows I'm on set all day. If he decides to turn up, then he turns up. Either way, contract or not, I refuse his services. Apparently, I'm in better hands with my driver."

"Absolutely not. You're right to refuse. I'm scratching his name from your contract now. After I send one of my best guys, who just came to the end of his contract with a different client, I'll let Leon know he's fired. As a way of apology, you'll get the next two months free."

"It's not necessary to give me free service. I can afford it, and people like sweet Clover need to be paid. Sending me a new guard is fine. Hopefully, this one cares if I end up dead."

"Don't worry at all. Timber is one of my highest requested guards. You'll love him."

He heard Maya take a deep breath. "Thank you. I appreciate your help. Do you mind transferring me back to Clover?"

A smile exploded across Saint's face. "No problem. It was good talking to you. You'll hear the phone start ringing again. Don't worry, it's sending you to Clover. Transferring now." Saint hit the button. He quickly sent texts to Timber and Leon. Then he rushed back out to Clover. Clover held the phone to his ear and smiled as if loving every word from Maya. "Please? I would absolutely love that."

Saint reclaimed his seat on Clover's desk. He chuckled as Clover stretched to put both gloved hands in front of the heater while holding the headset between his shoulder and ear. Saint pulled the heater closer and repositioned it to blow directly on Clover.

Clover flashed him a grateful smile that made it a little harder to breathe. He had never met anyone like this kitten.

After a few more minutes of back and forth, Clover hung up the phone. He was still smiling. "She's so nice. Thank you for helping her. I can't imagine how scared she must've been."

Saint was uncomfortable with praise. He simply dipped his chin. "Let's get out of here and go to lunch early. It's too damn cold to stay here."

Clover's smile turned fake. It was his turn to look uncomfortable. "Um. I've been out of work for a minute, and I live paycheck to paycheck. I can't really afford to go to lunch. Unfortunately, I'm counting every penny right now."

"That was me asking you to lunch. If I invite you, I'm paying." He stopped himself before adding he would pay, even if Clover did the inviting. That was just who he was.

"If you're sure." Clover did not sound like he could trust this offer. Saint should have been asking him that question.

"Yep. Transfer calls to the answering service and let's go."

Saint didn't wait to see if Clover complied. He knew he would. Saint needed to get his coat.

CHAPTER TWO

STRANGELY, CLOVER HAD NEVER been to the minuscule diner, just two doors down. He didn't spend a lot of time on the square. Thankfully, it was warm. He couldn't recall the last time he had been as miserable as he had been in that freezing office. While he had been raised here and was acclimated to the weather, he much preferred the heat. Not only was he cozy and warm now, but he had also decided Saint was the nicest person he had ever met.

He couldn't stop looking at all the bright holly, bells, and ornaments that were hanging around the diner. It was so pretty. He knew it was weird for him to love the season since he was completely alone.

"Kitten?"

"Yes?" Clover didn't know why he immediately answered to the pet name. He shouldn't encourage Saint. The guy had called him kitten three times during their lunch, pointing out his gloves and hat. *Three times*. That was all it had taken for that to become his name.

"What are you thinking about? It's like you disappeared inside your head."

"Would it be okay if I decorated the office for the holiday?"

Saint shrugged. "Knock yourself out. If you have time once Maya starts wearing out your phone, that is. Maya Heartland is a well-known talker. She'll make your ears tired."

Clover's jaw dropped. "You're joking. That was Maya Heartland? I love her! I didn't know she lived here. She my favorite sappy love movies' actress."

Saint's eyes flashed with good humor. "You seriously didn't know?"

Clover tried his ass off not to keep gushing. "No. When I answered the phone, she was somewhat hysterical, and I couldn't understand her at first. All I caught was the name Maya. There's no way I could've known it was *that* Maya.

Every Christmas, I curl up in an electric blanket with hot cocoa and cookies. I spend the entire day watching her holiday-themed movies. They're all basically the same, but I love them. They make me all warm inside." Clover snapped his teeth together. He couldn't believe he had said that.

Thankfully, Saint didn't call him on it. "She doesn't live here. It's a short-term contract she re-signs every time she's in town. She's filming three Christmas movies back-to-back here for release next year. Why are you alone on Christmas?"

It was like getting punched in the chest. He kept thinking it would get easier. It didn't.

Saint obviously saw something in his expression. "You don't have to answer that. In fact, I'll tell you why I'm alone." He didn't give Clover time to argue. "I was a runaway. When I was a teen, I left through my bedroom window and never looked back. Unfortunately, that meant I was homeless. One day, this huge motherfucker stepped into my path." A bright smile lit Saint's face. "Seriously, he was the biggest man I had ever seen. Just solid muscle. He asked if I was interested in a new life. A job and a fresh start. By that time, I was damn ready to get off the streets. So, without even knowing what I would be doing—even knowing it was likely drugs or sex—I said yes without a single moment's hesitation."

Clover heard the faked nonchalance to Saint's voice. He hated it. "My parents were deported seven years ago. I was born in the United States. I couldn't go with them, and they couldn't stay. Now they can't come, and I can't afford to go there." Clover shrugged, feeling uncomfortable. "So that's me." Clover set his elbow on the table and propped his chin up on his fist. "Why did you run away?"

"Terrible parents. That sort of thing."

"They say our past defines us. I've only known you a couple of hours, and you seem pretty great, so there's that," Clover added with a chuckle. He hated for Saint to think he flirted. Maybe he was. Even Clover didn't know. Saint just seemed so much like everything Clover had ever wanted for himself.

Saint opened his mouth to say God only knew what. The waitress appeared just in time to cut him off. The buxom blonde stayed completely focused on Saint. "Can I get you anything else?"

Saint looked up from stacking their plates. He focused on Clover. "I'm good. What about you, kitten? Do you want any dessert or anything?"

Clover couldn't look away from Saint. He couldn't believe Saint never even looked at the woman who had clearly fixed her blouse to show more cleavage since her last time around. She tried every trick, touching Saint's shoulder, and trying to take his coffee that he was still drinking. Nothing worked. Finally, Clover flashed her an uncomfortable smile, and she set the bill on the table.

When she walked away, Clover broke. "Holy crap. She wants you bad. You're killing her by not looking directly at her."

A line appeared between Saint's eyebrows. "Who?"

A laugh burst from Clover. "The waitress. She's fluffed her cleavage and everything."

Saint briefly glanced the woman's way. "Oh. She's not my type."

Clover was more than intrigued. "What is your type?"

Saint's gaze locked on him with an intensity Clover had never experienced. "You are."

Goddamn. Lust had never hit Clover as hard. He also would have never guessed that about Saint in a million years.

Some of his intensity vanished. "Please don't quit. I swear this isn't sexual harassment or anything. It's just you asked and—"

God, he was sweet. Clover had to stop his uncomfortable rambling. "I didn't take it personally. I put you on the spot. You answered the only way you could under the circumstances. I understand."

A sweet smile touched Saint's lips. "You really are incredible, you know? This is definitely the best hire I've ever made."

Clover felt his cheeks heat.

Saint's phone rang, saving Clover from having to come up with a response. He groaned when he saw the number. "This better not be them telling me they can't make it today. I can't have you freezing all day." He snatched up his phone and answered. "This is Saint." A smile touched his lips, making Clover fight back a sigh. "We'll head that way now. Thank you." Saint disconnected the call. He grabbed the bill and dropped some money on the table for a tip.

Clover was right on his heels as Saint headed to the counter to pay. Saint suddenly stopped. He pulled Clover next to him and set his hand on the small of Clover's back, steering him through the crowd. He genuinely made Clover feel so protected. Like conjuring up the devil, a couple shifted and Clover stared into Jacobe's cold eyes that were locked on him. Without thinking, Clover immediately stepped closer to Saint.

Saint glanced his way. "What's wrong?" He followed Clover's gaze. "Oh. There's a ballsy bastard. Jacobe?"

Clover nodded.

Saint squeezed him to his side while he paid. "Stay glued to me. I'd never let anything happen to you."

Clover nodded again. He couldn't get his throat to work. Clover could barely breathe. When would this end? Likely when he was dead.

Fucking enraged didn't cover the way Saint felt. He took Clover on a bit of a tour around the square. They didn't return to work until Saint was certain they weren't followed. Of course, it was entirely possible Jacobe was tracking Clover somehow. Saint would figure it out. Luckily, they got back to the office at the same time as the heat and air guy pulled into a parking spot. They could still see their breath when they came through the door.

Saint motioned toward his office. "Grab your heater and wait for me in there, kitten. Close the door behind you so we can trap as much heat as possible."

Clover nodded, looking defeated.

Saint hated that. "You're not in trouble. I just don't want to risk that guy walking by, peering into every glass surface and spotting you. Plus, we need to make a plan."

Clover nodded again. "Okay." He moved to his desk, gathered the heater, and rushed inside Saint's office. Saint pulled the door closed behind him while Clover searched for a free outlet.

The moment the door snapped shut, a repairman with "Rick" stitched on the right side of his chest stepped inside. Rick was all smiles.

"Mr. Knack?"

Saint dipped his chin. "That's me. You can call me Saint. Let me show you to that system."

Together, they headed to the back of the building. This was one of the biggest reasons he wanted Clover shut away in his office. He wouldn't risk Jacobe sailing into the building if he spotted Clover alone.

After pointing Rick to his job, Saint moved back to his office. As he grabbed the doorknob, his eyes quickly scanned the room, looking for anything suspicious. When he was certain they were alone, he stepped into the room and quickly closed the door behind him before they lost any heat. He found Clover cross-legged, knee bobbing, and biting the side of his thumbnail. This shit had to stop.

"We should have heat again in no time." Saint tried to keep his voice bright. He didn't like Clover being scared.

Clover flashed him a smile. "Great. Thank you for lunch, by the way." It was obvious he tried hiding his fear.

Saint sat behind his desk. "Did you drive here or take public transportation?"

Clover blinked at the sudden question. "Public transportation." He looked confused.

That didn't slow Saint. "Then he obviously doesn't have your car tagged. Do you have any trackers on you—like to find your keys, wallet, or phone?"

For a moment, Clover looked thoughtful before reaching into his coat pocket and pulling out keys. An AirTag inside a keychain hung from the keyring. "I have this."

Saint motioned for the keyring. Clover removed it from his keys and passed it over. He removed the keychain, popped out AirTag and removed the battery. Even though Clover never questioned him, Saint explained as he went. "This is likely how he keeps finding you. If he's ever had access to your phone, he could've easily unpaired this from your device and paired it with his. It literally takes seconds and then he can track your every move with you being none the wiser."

"I never thought about that. It's more than just likely. I lost my keys whenever we lived together. In my heart, I know he hid them from me. Then, suddenly, he appeared with them and that keychain so I wouldn't lose them again. I forgot all about that."

"Was he abusive?" Saint asked the question while putting the AirTag back together sans battery. He didn't want Clover feeling judged.

"Yes." Clover answered so quietly, Saint almost didn't hear him. His rage continued to build, but he refused to let Clover see it. He had obviously been through enough. Saint veered slightly off topic to give Clover time to recover from the confession.

He passed the battery-less keychain back to Clover. "The man I told you about who saved me from the streets, his name is

Steel. He owns the Steel Security brand. We have offices all over the U.S. where we have the heaviest business. To celebrate the holidays every year, he pays for all of us to travel to L.A. for a huge party on Christmas Eve. We usually get gifts and bonuses. It's a lot of fun. Since you're an employee now, that includes you." Saint took a breath. "If you're willing, I think you should stay with me until then and we can head to L.A. together." He took another deep breath, but Saint had to be honest. "I think you're in genuine danger. People don't keep stalking their exes for this long, normally. Combine that with him being abusive, tracking you, and the way I saw him look at you, I don't think you're safe alone. It's more than likely he'll strike sooner rather than later. We should be in control of that. If he thinks you're moving in with me, that'll likely be the straw that breaks him. I know what I'm suggesting is—"

"No," Clover said, cutting him off. "You're right. I can't keep living like this. It's really breaking me down."

It was a little scary how much hope filled Saint. He needed to keep things professional. "Does that mean you'll stay with me?"

Clover nodded. "If you're okay with me crashing on your couch or whatever, then I'm in."

Saint was helpless against his smile. "I get the feeling you like everyone you meet."

Clover blushed. "Not everyone."

"You're trusting me like you like me and have known me your whole life. You immediately took to Maya without realizing how famous she is. Not to mention, you were obviously concerned about our waitress' feelings."

"I'm just observant." The way Clover mumbled the words said a lot about how nervous he was.

Saint held his stare so Clover would see how serious he was. "I think you're great, kitten."

The small smile that met his words had Saint's heart trying to flip in his chest. He had a terrible feeling he was in big trouble, and he'd just invited that trouble home with him. Saint wasn't sure he was strong enough for this. He had to be. Clover was his employee. Ethics and all that. As he looked on, he watched Clover try to put the keychain back on his keys

with his tongue held between his teeth.
Jesus. He was fucked.

Chapter Three

It had taken forever at Clover's house for him to pack everything he needed for at least two weeks. Saint hadn't thought about how much stuff it took to make Clover so pretty. Apparently, it was a lot. Thankfully, they had gotten his things packed and in the back of Saint's SUV. Saint had gotten Clover settled into the spare bedroom and then left him to his shower. As much as Saint wanted to put his brain on lockdown, it wouldn't happen. Damn, Clover was brave and steady as hell. It was also possible he might be an idiot. Saint knew Clover could trust him. Hell, he had started at the bottom, doing guard duty at parties and whatnot before moving to watching over celebrities. Now he ran an entire branch of Steel Security. So, again, Saint knew he was safe, but Clover didn't. Yet he had come home with him, nonetheless. In his defense, though, Saint had seen his face when he spotted Jacobe. Maybe he was at a place in his life where he had found his breaking point. Anything at all felt safer than being alone. For fuck's sake, that motherfucker had been hired to be Clover's boss. Saint had dealt with some crazies in his line of work. One thing he knew was how to spot the ones who would kill someone before they let them go. Therefore, if staying with Saint was because he was brave or foolish, he was still safer here.

"Something smells delicious."

Saint turned away from the stove at Clover's statement. He barely stopped himself from blurting out how incredibly beautiful Clover was. Seriously, just drop-dead gorgeous. With his face free of makeup and wearing nothing more than a t-shirt and pajama shorts, he was flawless. His legs had Saint ready to worship them. Instead, he was forced to hold Clover's stare and pretend they were at work. This was only a business relationship.

"Thanks. It's chicken parmesan. Would you like to taste the sauce? I have a habit of putting in too much oregano. If you don't like it, I have more tomatoes. I can start over."

A gorgeous smile lit Clover's face. "Sure, but I love oregano. I'm sure it's fine."

Saint scooped some sauce from the pot with a wooden spoon and held it out for Clover to try. Clover claimed he loved oregano, but there was loving and there was LOVING, which was where Saint fell. It was possible he scorched away some of his tastebuds at some point.

Clover's eyes fell closed in pleasure. "Mhmm. That's exactly how I like it."

Saint couldn't look away from Clover, openly enjoying the sauce. Goddamn. Saint couldn't breathe. He had to clear his throat to speak. "Thank you. I'm usually too much for people." He let the statement hang in the air, hoping Clover understood he meant in every aspect of his life.

Clover grabbed a nearby stool and sat next to the oven. "I think you're perfect." His words were so nonchalant, Saint couldn't get a read on him. Saint didn't even know why he tried. This was strictly a professional relationship. Surely, if he kept telling himself that, he could make it real. Except Saint knew the truth. He could tell himself that all day, but in the end, Saint couldn't pretend he would have done this for any newbie hire. He was incapable of letting Clover out of his sight.

Clover straightened his spine and clasped his hands. "Now. I have a serious question."

"Shoot."

Clover didn't hesitate. "Do you hate Christmas?"

"Why?" He very much feared he knew exactly why, but he wouldn't volunteer anything if he wasn't asked directly.

Clover motioned wildly. "You have zero decorations. It's one thing to not decorate the office. This is a new level."

So much for not volunteering any information. He didn't want to make Clover think he was a Scrooge or whatever. He stared down at his hands as he worked on their meal. Really, there wasn't much left to do. He just didn't want to see any pity on Clover's face. "When I said I left through the window because of terrible parents, I left out it wasn't my parents' house. It was my aunt's. That's who I was placed with after my dad murdered my mom before killing himself on Christmas."

Clover gasped.

Saint kept talking. He still didn't want to see Clover's expression. "They always fought. Since they were both alcoholics, they usually got pretty violent. When I was little, I would hide until it was over, which was usually when they passed out. When I got a little older, I would leave and stay gone for a few hours. That's what I did that Christmas." He shrugged. "I came home and found them. There was blood everywhere, soaking the one present I actually had under the tree. For a little while, after I went to live with my aunt, it was like I was in shock. I didn't notice much of anything around me. Then I started to slowly realize my aunt was just the same: a mean drunk. So I left. When

Steel found me, I needed the money. But then I stayed on because I needed to protect other people. I've seen insanity and what it can do. If I can stop it in some way, I will."

"Holy shit. I'm sorry. Don't worry. I won't decorate the office."

Saint smiled. He couldn't help but meet Clover's stare. "No. You're good. Go wild. You can even decorate here, if you'd like. I think you're the kind of person who can create happy memories. If you're willing, I'd like that."

Clover beamed. "I can do that."

Saint gave him a sharp nod. "Tomorrow, after work, we'll hit the store and one of those Christmas tree lots."

"Okay." The happiness in Clover's voice let Saint know he had made the right decision. He had also been serious. Saint liked the idea of making happy memories with Clover. He couldn't think of a better way to spend the holiday.

The day had definitely been a series of highs and lows. At the end of it all, there had been way more highs than lows. Unfortunately, the downward path had been extremely rocky. He still couldn't believe he had accidentally forced Saint to relive such an atrocious memory, but Clover felt like he knew Saint better now. He understood what motivated him to bring Clover home with him. Maybe now he could stop imagining Saint looked at him with hunger in his eyes. Maybe he was just a little lonely. He was super excited to plan a holiday with Saint. Saint wasn't the only one who needed someone to help him push through. Clover hated to admit how much he had come to dread going home. He knew Christmas would be even worse this year, with Jacobe popping up everywhere. Clover didn't put it past him to try to capitalize on his holiday depression.

After the best dinner he'd had in a long time, Clover washed dishes with Saint at his side. He was honestly pretty wiped after such a wild day. But he was oddly reluctant to move away from Saint and he couldn't say why. He hadn't felt so immediately attached to anyone in his life. He was just comfortable, as if they had been friends his entire life. It was nice.

He released the water and wiped down the sink. As much as he hated it, there was no pushing off his exhaustion. "Well, I guess I should get to bed now. I don't really sleep well. Being in a new place, it might take me longer than usual."

"Do you need me to tuck you in and read you a bedtime story?"

A bark of laughter burst from Clover at the unexpected remark. He couldn't look away from the way Saint's eyes swam with laughter. "Does that actually work? I've only ever seen it done in movies."

Saint shrugged. "All I own is smut, but we could still try it and find out."

The loud guffaw that left him had Clover covering his nose and mouth, trying to stifle the sound. He had never had so much fun. He swiped at his eyes. "Um. I'm not sure smut would have me sleeping comfortably."

The way Saint laughed kept Clover smiling. He didn't want to walk away. Clover took a step back. "I guess I should really go to bed."

Saint must have seen the reluctance in him. "Or we could turn out the lights and watch some old movies. I'll get out the electric blanket for you. If you fall asleep, I'll just carry you to bed."

The way his body reacted to picturing himself in Saint's arms was a little horrifying. The longing that hit was like nothing he had ever experienced. He couldn't force himself to say no.

"That sounds fantastic."

He was pretty sure their smiles matched as they headed to the living room together. Saint's house was actually a cabin. Gorgeous trees surrounded the place. He couldn't say why, but the moment he saw the place, Clover had immediately thought, *This screams Saint*. It was the perfect home for him. Even though it was a small house with only two bedrooms and two bathrooms, the rooms were pretty big. The entire place was also immaculate. Clover wondered if that was due to Saint's homelessness back in the day. Maybe it made him take extra pride in owning a home or something. No matter the reason, he still felt at home. It was as if the cabin was every bit as welcoming as its owner.

Clover sat on the couch and curled his feet underneath him. He watched as Saint plugged in the blanket, set it on medium, and covered him. Clover was immediately cozy. He wanted to snuggle deeper.

"What would you like to watch? I have so many streaming channels, I can likely find anything that comes to mind."

The question made Clover want to compare their tastes. "How about Lord of the Rings?"

A bright smile lit Saint's face. "Fuck yeah. I love those movies."

"And the TV series," they said simultaneously.

They shared a smile.

Saint sat close to him as he went through the process of pulling up the movie. Clover turned sideways so he could openly stare. "I can't believe how much we have in common. It's like we've been friends for years."

Saint lifted Clover's feet into his lap and shared the blanket. He massaged Clover's feet as he looked Clover's way. His expression was serious. No more laughter. "It does feel that way, doesn't it? I'm glad we met."

Clover couldn't help his tiny sigh of contentment. "Me too."

For a moment, they held each other's stare before the beginning notes of the movie starting had them looking away. Clover wasn't sure what was happening, but whatever it was, he wanted it.

CHAPTER FOUR

DAY TWO OF HIS new job went even better than he hoped. Saint had been right about Maya. Clover had given her his cellphone number, and she texted him several times during the day. She was also one of those who had to send the last text in every conversation, even if it was just hearts. He had picked that one up pretty quickly and just let her have it. Clover liked her a lot. He was happy to hear the new guard Saint had sent did a better job of protecting her.

On the other end of the spectrum, he had barely set eyes on Saint. Nothing had seemed wrong this morning. Clover had woken up tucked into bed. Maybe he had snored too loudly. Saint hadn't seemed any different at breakfast. He was over-thinking every little thing. Clover knew Saint had been busy. He had been the one transferring nonstop calls to him all day. Him not asking if he could help people made zero difference. Everyone still told him everything before he sent them Saint's way. Those chats had made him realize exactly how much Saint dealt with every day. He had clients calling, em-ployees calling, and new contracts in the works. Saint must run the entire north. He had no idea how Saint had done

Clover's job and his too. Clover was tired just thinking about it.

While Clover was lost in thought, Saint appeared. He knocked on Clover's desk. "Hey, kitten. You ready to get that tree?"

The happiness that ran through Clover at the sight of Saint was off the charts. He had to swallow it down. "I've been thinking about the tree." Clover stood as he talked and grabbed his coat. Saint took it from him and helped him into his fluffy jacket. Clover let it happen like they did this every day. "We'll be leaving for a week, and live trees are highly flammable. Plus, we can reuse a fake tree every year. Of course, we also need to pick up decorations. It's like one-stop shopping."

Saint wore a huge grin. "You could've stopped at *we'll* use it every year."

Clover hadn't realized he had said that. The entire speech just rolled off his tongue. "I mean..."

Saint shook his head and took Clover's hand as they headed for the door. "Nope. No takesies backsies. You're officially tied to me for life. We'll co-own a tree. We practically have a kid now."

Clover couldn't stop laughing. Saint was like starting over—like fresh air. He made Clover feel things. Clover never wanted to be away from him again. His laughter died when they reached Saint's SUV. Even though fat snowflakes fell from the sky and had slightly begun piling on the ground, there was no missing the carnage. Three of his tires had been slashed, and the SUV had been keyed in several places. Everything inside Clover froze in terror. Not only about Jacobe, but Saint wouldn't want to be his friend anymore after this. They wouldn't buy a tree together. No one wanted to be near someone who brought this to their life. Soon, he would be alone again. Tears filled his eyes. Then he found his face squashed against Saint's solid chest. It was like he tried to protect Clover from every angle while still having his phone against his ear. Clover couldn't understand a single word. He was having a major panic attack. Nothing made sense.

Then Saint's arms were around him. He stroked Clover's back. "It's okay. Just breathe."

Clover didn't even realize he was crying. He was definitely getting makeup all over Saint's shirt. "This is my fault. If you'd never met me..."

Saint kissed his head and didn't move away. He spoke against Clover's skin. "I don't feel that way at all. It's impossible for me to find the words to explain right now. I know it doesn't make sense, but you're the best thing that's happened to me in a long time. Everything else is just noise."

Clover's heart rate slowed. He realized he had Saint's shirt held tightly in his fists. He still didn't let go, but he got himself under control. Saint smelled so good. Manly. Clover took a deep breath. "You're the best thing too." He didn't expound. Clover didn't know how to say Saint was the best thing that had ever happened to him. Full stop. "I'm scared as hell you won't want to be stuck co-parenting a tree with me now."

He felt Saint's chuckle.

Screeching tires had Clover's heart jumping into his throat. Saint didn't release him until voices joined them. Clover turned to find some of the largest men he had ever seen in his life. He didn't realize how hard he shook until Saint no longer held him.

Saint molded against Clover's back and wrapped the two halves of his coat around Clover, trapping him in the warmth against his chest. Clover didn't bat an eyelash. It felt exactly like something Saint would do. He was a protective bear. Plus, he was certain he was where he should be.

Almost all the guys moved toward them while the others moved to deal with Saint's SUV. They all looked dangerous. A large flatbed tow truck worked to tilt its bed, obviously getting ready to haul away

Saint's vehicle. Several people spoke to him, wearing huge smiles and talking about how they had spoken on the phone today. Clover tried to hang on to their names. He had a bad feeling his smile looked every bit as brittle as it felt, and he could barely focus on their words. Someone quietly spoke to Saint, but he could barely keep up with the men bombarding him, much less what Saint said.

"Two tags." Everyone turned toward the guy who made the announcement. He held up two AirTags. All the guys moved toward the SUV.

"They weren't there last night. I checked."

Clover didn't recall seeing Saint check, but he likely hadn't wanted Clover to worry. Saint probably knew some trick to check for that type of thing on the sly.

The men went to work, getting the vehicle ready to be taken away, and pulling up video footage from all the cameras Clover didn't know they had.

Saint pressed his lips against the shell of his ear. "If he's out there watching, I want him to see how many people are protecting you. I want him to see us like this and think we're together. Boss and employee will only lead to more of him searching the local businesses. If he believes we're more, he'll turn his fury on me." He motioned toward the SUV. "Exhibit A."

Clover nodded. "I get it, but I couldn't live with myself if you got hurt because of me."

A light kiss skimmed his ear. Even more goosebumps skirted his skin. Clover knew it was all an act, but fuck. His greedy heart begged for more.

"I can take it. Remember, this used to be my job. I know how to protect myself."

White-hot jealousy slapped Clover. He had done this with clients. Clover had to talk himself down. This was dumb. Saint wasn't his.

The guard who Clover actually remembered came to hover close. His name was Diesel. Clover remembered that because of his size. He was tall and massive—like a diesel truck.

Diesel kept his voice low. "We've got the truck ready to go and all the video footage to analyze. I'm leaving the Ram for you. I'll catch a ride with Marc."

"Sounds good. Thanks for coming so quickly."

After Saint and Diesel did some sort of manly clasping of hands thing, Diesel's gaze moved his way. He was all smiles. "It really is great to finally put a face to the voice." He focused on Saint once more. "He's definitely a keeper. Best office manager you've ever had."

Clover's cheeks heated. He didn't know why the compliment made him suddenly so uncomfortable with praise, but it did. "Thank you."

Diesel glanced his way and waved away Clover's words. "It's the truth." He switched his gaze to Saint again. "I'll get out of your way now so you can get this one out of the cold. We'll stay behind and make sure you're not followed."

"Thanks. I always appreciate you."

With Saint's goodbyes out of the way, he released Clover but stayed glued to his back until he got Clover ushered into the truck. It was nice and warm already. Clover watched Saint circle the front of the truck and climb behind the wheel. He was incapable of looking away.

Saint met his stare as he pulled his door closed. "Let's go adopt that tree."

The smile that exploded across his face was out of his control. He wished like hell he could stay like this forever. Clover was pretty sure he had met the one and they would never be together.

It turned out Saint loved spending money on Clover, much to Clover's open horror. It took them forever to get everything into the house. He had spent several hundred dollars on groceries alone. Saint didn't want Clover to go hungry. Plus, they needed snacks for their night of decorating. Damn. Saint really felt like he never had before, and he couldn't stop noticing every time Clover looked at him the same. He was positive it wasn't just his imagination. The way Clover had let him hold him and kiss his ear, not just anyone would have let him get away with that. While one could claim Clover had just gone along with the plan of protection, Saint had felt the way Clover's breathing had changed. They were in trouble because they definitely wanted each other.

Saint had also bought a tree and a fuck-ton of decorations. They needed some for the office too. Several times, Clover had tried to give him money. That wasn't happening. Saint always paid, especially knowing how much Clover needed to hang on to every dime. He had to spoil Clover. Saint couldn't stop.

With all the bags inside, Saint focused on Clover. "Why don't you go ahead and do what you need to do to get ready to be in for the night. I'll put all this up."

Clover huffed. "First you paid and now you also want to do all the work?"

Saint kept his expression blank. "Do you know where any of this goes?"

Clover chewed his bottom lip for a second. Then he brightened. "I could unpack all the decorations."

"Absolutely not. We're supposed to do that together."

At his reminder, Clover's hands rose and fell. "All right, then. I'll try to take a quicker shower than usual."

Saint shook his head. "Don't rush. I have to get my pajamas on too, so we can do this right. So take all the time you need. I'm not going anywhere."

Clover looked resigned, but he nodded and headed down the hall.

Saint nearly sighed in relief. He had a lot of secret stuff to do and very little time to do it. Saint put up groceries at the speed of light before he rushed to the bedroom to change. The shower still ran in Clover's room, so he threw a batch of marshmallow-topped hot chocolate to-gether. While that heated, he hid the gift he had bought on the sly. He slipped it into his halfway packed suitcase so he wouldn't forget it. Saint was back in time to stir the cocoa and pour two mugs. With precision timing, Clover padded into the kitchen, wearing some sort of one-piece Christmas pajamas. It had little footies and zipped in the front. There was barely any skin showing and Saint was still more aroused than he could recall ever being. He was glad he wore a long shirt. No way were his thin pajama pants hiding his erection. The shirt probably wasn't doing much either.

"You're adorable."

Clover didn't blush like he had a tendency to do. He boldly held Saint's stare. His expression gave nothing away. "I could say the same of you, but I'm afraid you wouldn't appreciate it."

The claim surprised a laugh from Saint. "Why wouldn't I appreciate it?"

Clover's smile made an appearance. "Your manly image might be hurt by getting called adorable."

Saint shook his head and passed Clover his cup of hot chocolate. "I guess we should get this tree set up."

Clover didn't look bothered by Saint skimming over his compliment. Saint still wasn't certain this was the best idea. He grew closer to Clover every minute they were together. Saint felt like he had a new best friend. A best friend he wanted to fuck... who also worked for him. An aggravated growl ran through Saint's head. He couldn't help how he felt. There was no stopping the march of his heart toward Clover.

Clover followed on his heels to the living room. "The tree we picked is pretty big. Where should we put it?"

Saint eyed the room. He motioned toward the window. "I can move that chest from underneath the window to the corner. Then that would give us the perfect spot. You know, like it looks on Christmas cards. Lights peeking through a fogged-up window as snow falls outside. That kind of thing."

Clover stared at him in a way he couldn't decipher. "You're really getting to this, huh?"

He was because Clover was there. Clover's joy for the holiday was catching. Plus, for the first time, he felt like he had someone to share Christmas with. He wasn't alone.

"I promised I'd give this a real shot."

Clover took a drink. "Holy shit. That's delicious." He set the cup aside. "You move the chest. I'll open the box."

"Sounds good." Saint passed him the pocketknife he had held on to for just this purpose after changing.

Together, they got to work. They worked so seamlessly together, it was like they had done this every year for years. He didn't remember half of what they talked about. It was mostly chatting about their lives and laughing. So much laughing. That was the one thing Saint couldn't get past. He wanted this to be his life. He was too old to join the dating world. The last thing Saint wanted to do was try to keep up with some club hopper who would want an open relationship. Saint just wanted this. A comfortable life with someone who made everything brighter. Something real and built on friendship.

"Well. There's nothing left but the mistletoe." Clover turned in a circle. "Where should we hang it?"

There was already a small hook where he used to have a hanging plant. Instead of answering, Saint lifted Clover over his head.

A loud laugh burst from Clover. It died when he obviously spotted the hook. "Oh. That's perfect."

Saint couldn't think. He hadn't really considered his actions until he realized how close Clover's dick was to his face. It got a little harder to breathe.

"There."

Saint slowly lowered Clover, letting his body slide down Saint's body. The air in the room changed. When Clover was on his feet, his arms were still around Saint's neck. They didn't look away from each other.

Saint broke first. "Someone needs to break it in." He didn't think. Saint touched his lips to Clover's. He honestly thought if he ever threw away all good sense and did this, he would probably end up ripping off Clover's clothes. Instead, the kiss was slow and sexy. Saint held Clover like he was every bit as precious as he was. They equally kept their hands respectful. Saint still lost his entire soul. By the time Saint pulled away, he couldn't catch his breath, and his dick was beyond hard. It was begging. Clover didn't open his eyes right away, nor did he step out of Saint's hold. When his eyes opened, he looked sultry and kind of like he was lost in the passion.

"I think the mistletoe works."

Saint smiled so hard, his face hurt at Clover's claim. "It seems so."

Clover visibly swallowed. "I guess I should get to bed."

Saint nodded. "That's probably for the best."

Even though it killed him, Saint let his arms drop. They shared another longing glance before Clover walked away.

CHAPTER FIVE

SAINT HAD BARELY SLEPT. Unfortunately, running an office didn't care if he was tired. He dragged himself from bed and got in the shower. The hot water didn't clear his mind. In fact, the temperature made his eyelids heavier. Then it hit Saint. Clover was still here. The faster he got ready, the quicker he would see him. Saint ended up rushing through the motions and tossing on some clothes. He knew it had been snowing, so he dressed appropriately. It was supposed to have snowed all night and would continue for the next three days. But this was Washington and part of life. They all just got on with it.

He found Clover already at the kitchen table with a cream cheese bagel and coffee. "Hey."

Clover's chipper greeting weakened Saint's knees. He had panicked all night that things would be weird now.

Clover motioned toward the counter. "I heard you rustling around, so I made you coffee and a bagel too."

Saint eyed the breakfast Clover had put together. By sight alone, it looked as if his coffee was the right color. He took a sip to be sure so he wouldn't have to backtrack from the table if it wasn't right.

It was perfect. Clover had doctored it exactly the way Saint liked it.

"I'm always blown away by how you take care of me. You even got my coffee right."

Clover smiled as he watched Saint carry his breakfast to the table. "We've spent a lot of time together the last few days. You always order your coffee the same."

Saint held up his cream cheese-slathered bagel. "This is great too. How did you know this is how I like my bagels?"

Clover chuckled. "You bought bagels and cream cheese. I just put two and two together. You're also just like me when it comes to excess of everything flavorful. So I risked that you like a lot of cream cheese."

Saint shook his head. Every day, he got a little more addicted. "Watch out. I might have to keep you."

Clover laughed, but he didn't say no.

Saint couldn't stop reading into every tiny detail. He couldn't shake the feeling they had known each other in another life.

They sat in companionable silence. Saint fully recognized they dragged their feet a bit. A few minutes late wouldn't matter. Once they were finally ready to head out the door, they both stamped into winter boots.

Saint opened the door. He froze. The bright white snow combined with the sun beating on it to blind him. Also, it was all the way to his stomach and shaped the outline of the door.

They exchanged a glance. Neither of them wanted to dive into that mess.

"I'll call and have the answering service take all our calls and have emergencies sent here."

Clover nodded.

Saint shut the door.

They didn't look away from each other.

Saint had no idea who moved first, but they came together like waves crashing against the bluffs. He tore off his coat before shoving Clover's down his arms. They kicked their way out of their boots without ever pulling away from their kiss. The moment Saint was out of his, he swept Clover off his feet. Clover wrapped his legs around Saint's waist. Saint had him down the hall so fast, he didn't remember the trip. He tossed Clover onto the bed. Under any other circumstances, Saint might have laughed at how Clover still wore one boot. The lust that stared back at him shot his ego through the roof. He quickly pulled the boot from Clover's foot and tossed it aside.

While still holding Clover's stare, he pulled his shirt up and over his head. Saint blindly threw it in the direction of the boot.

Clover's gaze swept down Saint's body. The arousal written all over his face doubled. He rolled upward and took off his shirt.

Saint damn near swallowed his tongue. Not only did he have a body only made at the gym, but a large panther tattoo also covered one side of his chest and shoulder.

"Goddamn." Saint couldn't stop the curse. He honestly had no expectations. Saint had barely thought about what might be under Clover's clothes. He had been horny as fuck over Clover's personality alone, but the guy was just... whoa. No wonder he had some guy ready to go to prison for his crazy methods of stalking him. Saint might do the same if Clover walked away, except he would be much better at it. Clover wasn't getting away from him.

He had to know more. Saint reached for the button on Clover's jeans. His gaze collided with Clover's beautiful brown eyes. "You can tell me to stop. I will."

Clover never broke eye contact. "Not only will you not hear that from me, but I'm silently begging you to hurry."

That was all Saint needed to hear.

He changed his mind and tore his way out of his pants before going to work on Clover's. In record time, they were nude. Just holy hell. Saint had to cover Clover's body with his to keep from tearing into him. He had never been this turned on. Then again, he had also never felt this strongly about anyone. It was almost like they had built something before the sex and now he was a fucking goner.

Their mouths clashed. They had surpassed worrying about working together. They were hunger and need.

Clover tore his mouth away. "Damn. You feel so good on top of me."

Saint nipped at Clover's neck before responding. "That's because you belong underneath me." He paused for a moment. "Not that I wouldn't love being beneath you too. Goddamn." Clover fried Saint's brain. "Tell me how you like it. I'm up for anything." Literally.

Clover panted for air before answering. "I want you inside me."

Fuck yeah. Saint didn't ask questions. He dove for a condom and lube. Saint really hoped the condom was still in date. Did they go bad? It had been a damn long time. He would be damned if he started swiping right. Saint still remembered exactly how to get someone ready to be fucked. He put all his skill into that now. While licking a very sexy set of abs, Saint worked between Clover's thighs. He rolled the condom on before wetting his fingers. Saint went slow, circling Clover's asshole.

"You're killing me." The way pre-cum leaked onto Clover's stomach screamed that was the truth. Clover's hips lifted as if seeking more.

Saint pushed his fingers inside and pumped. He made sure Clover was stretched and ready before curling his fingers and massaging.

Clover moaned.

The sound damn near made Saint blow. He couldn't wait any longer. Saint held Clover's desperate stare as he probed Clover's wet hole. He slipped inside an inch.

Clover looked like the porn channel with the way he reacted.

Saint lost the battle. He slammed into Clover. His vision darkened. Saint had to pause there. Heaven swallowed him. If he didn't take a breath, he would come. No way was Clover walking away from to-day thinking he was a two-pump chump.

Only when he was certain he had himself under control did he try again. He slipped nearly all the way from Clover's ass. Then he thrust.

Damn near all of Clover's body left the bed when his back bowed. He looked like he had never had so much plea-sure. It was addicting. Clover's every re-action fascinated him. Saint couldn't tear his eyes away as Clover writhed beneath him. He was the sexiest thing Saint had ever seen. Clover was also making it hard as hell to hold out.

"I've never seen anyone more beautiful."

Clover didn't respond. He didn't stop trying to take his pleasure, proving he wasn't faking. The knowledge made him crazed. He pumped and changed angles until the sounds Clover made sounded more desperate. Saint kept the rhythm. He felt Clover tense. The guy nearly crippled him. He wasn't going to make it. Clover felt too good. Then cum shot from Clover and his body had Saint seeing stars.

"Holy shit, Clover. You're perfect. Do you want to get married? I'd give you everything." Saint's mouth simply ran without his brain. He was too close. Saint pumped faster and harder. The building pressure had him holding his breath. His entire body jerked. Inhuman sounds came from deep inside his throat. Saint gasped for air while still trying to kiss any place he could while riding out the world's largest orgasm. With a mess of cum and sweat everywhere, Saint molded against Clover and kissed him like how he felt: too much. Even as his body and mind cooled, none of his needy thoughts changed. Saint wanted to keep this man. No matter what it took.

Clover's body ached but also hummed with pleasure. His mind was all sunshine and rainbows. He had known they would be good together. They equally showed too much of their hearts every time they looked at each other. Passion had boiled under the surface since the first five minutes they met. Clover couldn't define it, but it was just an immediate certainty they belonged together. Logically, he had recognized every second that they had never even pretended to be boss and employee. That interview had felt more like a blind date that was magical and binding.

Saint sat on the edge of the bed, still nude. Unfortunately, he dealt with an emergency call. Clover ran his fingertip down Saint's spine, lightly stroking each bump. He couldn't stop. Clover adored the way his touch brought chill bumps to the surface of Saint's skin. Saint's body fascinated Clover. He was very much a bear. Just as Clover had thought since the first moment they met. He was huge and burly. Perfect for protecting people. He took up all the space. Clover had never felt safer in his life.

Saint finished his call and tossed his phone aside before settling back down to cuddle.

Clover used his arm as a pillow.

Saint kissed his head. "I let everyone know the office will be closed the rest of the week, and—of course—next week too, for Christmas. This snow won't melt overnight. Oh, and don't worry. You'll still get paid."

Clover nodded, but his gaze stayed locked on Saint's beautiful eyes.

A hint of worry appeared in his eyes as Clover looked on. "I don't want you to worry about your job." He motioned between them. "This is something I can't explain, but I don't want me being your boss to be part of it. I don't know what I'm trying to say. Just please don't think less of me. I realize you might feel like there's a power imbalance. There isn't. I just really like you and—"

"I'm not worried," Clover said, cutting off Saint's babbling. "With anyone else, I'd probably feel differently, but this is different. Logically, I know you're my boss, but it's never felt like that's all you are. Now I'm the one having a hard time voicing what I mean. We just fit."

Saint rolled to his side, facing Clover and pulled Clover closer. Clover draped his leg over Saint's hip. Saint stole a quick kiss before going back to holding his stare. "I don't know what happened. It doesn't make sense, but I genuinely feel something for you."

Clover nodded. "Same."

"According to the forecast, it is supposed to warm up dramatically over the weekend. I'm hoping that means the snow won't affect our flight. Not that I'm complaining about being snowed in with you."

"Whether it's in California or we're still right here, I'm looking forward to a solid week and a half of having you in bed."

The hunger in Saint's expression made Clover's stomach do a weird kind of flop. He wanted more.

"This is the life I've always wanted. Am I scaring you yet?"

Clover didn't back down at the confession. "No. I've always wanted this too. We definitely have chemistry, but I feel comfortable. At peace. Does that make sense? Are you scared now?" Clover wasn't truly worried, considering how big Saint's smile had gotten.

"Not at all. In fact, I'd like to hear more about this chemistry."

Heat flowed from Clover. He knew it had to show in his expression. "Sure. I've never wanted anyone so instantly in my life." Clover's gaze dropped to Saint's lips for a second before meeting his stare again. "You are just... damn." The curse came out sounding like pure desire.

Saint rolled, pinning Clover beneath him. He kissed the corner of Clover's mouth. "Don't worry. I won't hurt you. I know you have to be sore, but I will make you fly." As Saint's tongue filled his mouth, Clover prayed they never got each other out of their systems. He wanted this for life. Clover would do anything it took to hold on to them.

CHAPTER SIX

WHITE CHRISTMAS LIGHTS LIT up the room. Saint swore Clover twinkled as he moved from person to person, getting to know everyone. He was definitely a social butterfly who seemed to never meet a stranger. In under a minute, he charmed everyone he met. Saint couldn't look away.

Clover wore a light gray soft outfit that had silver threading through it. That was likely the reason he seemed to catch the light and reflect it. The bow-neck shirt kept sliding down his shoulder, exposing part of his tattoo. He was stunning.

"Do I need to worry about the way you're looking at your new office manager?"

Saint didn't exactly jump at Steel's sudden appearance at his side. But he had definitely been lost in the vision Clover created. Saint lifted his beer to his lips to buy himself a moment before speaking.

"I guess it depends."

A soft, tired-sounding sigh left Steel. "I feel like I'll regret asking this, but on what?"

Saint hid a smile. Despite his earlier harsh tone, Steel was a softy. "It depends on if you're okay with the fact that we're a couple." He met Steel's eyes that matched his name. "This isn't a fling. He isn't just some guy."

Steel's closed expression didn't waver as his gaze slid Clover's way. "He's personable. I'll give him that." Steel hesitated before adding, "And beautiful. Just answer something else for me. Did you give your man a job or did you jump your employee?" Steel made a wild gesture. "Don't answer that. I don't want to know. It's better if I pretend whatever I want to believe is the truth."

A quiet chuckle sneaked out. Sometimes, Steel could be funny as hell. Before he could say anything, Clover joined them. A half second before Saint heard him, he felt him. His gaze snapped in Clover's direction.

Clover was still all smiles as he slipped his hand into the crook of Saint's arm. He was focused on Steel.

"This is truly an amazing party. Thank you for inviting me, even though this is only my second week working for the company."

Steel looked every bit as smitten with Clover as everyone did. He made a dismissive gesture. "Don't worry. Everyone is family here, no matter how long they've been with me. Plus, everyone has sung your praises since you came onboard. Hell, Maya Heartland called to tell me how good you were to her in a moment of crisis. That's exactly what we need. Compassion matters when people are at their lowest."

Clover looked moved. "Thank you for that, but I don't think anyone could've heard the terror in Maya's voice and dismissed it. She could've been killed. Any number of horrible things might've happened to her."

Steel never looked away from Clover. It was like Saint had vanished. "Exactly. It's obvious you truly care. We need more of that."

Clover nodded. "I'll admit this position has been way more fulfilling than I expected. It feels like I'm actually helping people."

"You are." Steel's fast response was filled with honesty. Another man felled by the magic that was Clover. Steel glanced around. "I suppose I should give my speech and hand out gifts before people get too drunk and restless."

Clover laughed. "Hold on just a second." He dipped his hand into the pocket of Saint's dress coat. Saint knew he carried something for Clover, but he hadn't bothered to check what it was. Clover popped open a tube normally used to carry cuff links to keep them safe. He shook out a pin. "A little birdie told me you love all things dogs." He clipped the golden pin on the lapel of Steel's dress coat. "There. In my parents' home country, dogs are considered a symbol of good luck, loyalty, and protection. In this case, that little golden puppy makes your entire outfit complete." Clover stepped back and reclaimed Saint's arm.

Steel seemed more moved than Saint ever would have dreamed over such a small gesture. The guy was loaded in a way most people couldn't even fathom. Yet a tiny gold pin looked as if it was the perfect gift to Steel.

"Thank you. You have no idea how much I love it."

Clover beamed as Steel moved to the small stage set up for the event.

Pride filled him as he stared at Clover. He was literally the best person Saint had ever met. Saint would do right by him. Clover would see.

Clover tried to keep a calm demeanor while jumping for joy inside. His bonus from Steel had more zeros than he ever expected. Plus, everyone had been so, so welcoming and nice. Jacobe, going as far as getting a job to be his boss, turned out to be the best blessing in disguise. As scared as he had been to change employers, somehow he had managed to find his dream position. He felt over the moon. Clover knew a big part of that was Saint. He chewed on the side of his nail as he waited for Saint to finish getting ready for bed. Clover had already showered and climbed into bed naked. There was no way he could fall asleep without Saint.

Saint padded from the bathroom, totally nude, making Clover nearly swallow his tongue. Saint was all man. He made Clover hot as hell.

As he looked on, Saint's dick stirred.

Saint growled. "Don't look at me like that. I won't let you sleep tonight."

"Mmm, sexy. Don't threaten me with a good time."

Saint's open toiletries bag sat on the nightstand. That was where the condoms and lube were. Saint dug inside the bag.

Clover's cock throbbed.

Saint came out with a tiny gift box. "Merry Christmas."

A wave of something powerful washed over him. He sat up, letting the covers slide into his lap. "Wait. I have something for you too." He leaned over to get it from his bedside table.

Saint stopped him. "Please open this first."

Since it seemed important, Clover accepted the box. Even though it looked wrapped, it was actually in two pieces. Clover could lift the lid without unwrapping it. He could only blink when he stared into the open box. It took him a second to realize the reason he couldn't see clearly was the tears in his eyes.

"It's beautiful." His voice cracked. He was much closer to crying than he cared to admit. Saint always moved him. He was perfect.

Saint climbed into bed and lifted the necklace from the gift box. He easily undid the clasp and put the gorgeous piece of jewelry around Clover's neck.

Clover stroked the row of diamonds that fell down his chest in a straight line, twinkling against his skin. "I love it."

Clover sniffed and grabbed Saint's present before he actually broke down. "Here. Open yours. I'll explain as you do." He handed the folder to Saint. "You know how we stayed up talking all night for like three nights in a row?"

Saint laughed. "Yeah. I'm pretty sure my days and nights are flip-flopped now. After spending each morning making love to you, I'm also pretty sure I'll get a hard-on every morning at exactly nine now."

Clover couldn't stop smiling. "I'll be sure to check. But anyhow, you told me when you were a kid, you wanted to be a race car driver. I learned one of your clients is famous for just that. When we spoke on the phone, he offered to let me take a spin around the track. I told him I'm gay. Has he ever been in a Trader Joe's parking lot? We're a menace. Anyhow, he laughed, and I had an idea. I told him my boss was a great driver and had always wanted to get out on the track. Then I asked if you could take that spin instead of me." He tapped on the folder Saint still hadn't opened. "It turns out it's a very official thing they do for rich people and sponsors. So he sent me the formal invitation along with some paperwork you have to fill out. But this spring, you have a date with a very fast car."

Saint never looked away from him while Clover spoke. A huge smile lit his face. "This is amazing. I can't believe you did this." He flipped open the folder and his eyes practically bugged out of his head. "Forty-eight minutes of track time. Do you have any idea how much this costs? I know exactly which client you mean, and this is the highest package you can get. You must've really made an impression on him."

Clover made a dismissive gesture. "All it took was me offering to sleep with him."

Saint's expression turned harder than Clover had ever seen.

He rushed to fix it. "I'm only joking. Maya is sending me an autographed photo to give him. All I have to do is meet her for lunch to pick it up when we get back, which I planned to do anyhow."

Saint rubbed his chest. "Please don't do that again. I lost five years off my life." He set the folder aside.

Clover's shoulders fell. "You don't like that I bartered for your gift. I was worried about that. At the time, I couldn't afford to buy you anything special enough to suit my heart. I didn't know I would get this bonus. If you want, I can turn down his offer and buy you something else. Something more like what you gave me."

Saint ran his hand down Clover's arm before linking fingers with him. "No. That's not what I meant at all. It was you even joking about sleeping with someone else. That would break my heart. As for the gift, it's perfect. It's not about the price. You definitely got me something from the heart. No one else has ever considered my wants before. I absolutely love it."

Clover stared at their joined hands. He swallowed, but no matter how hard he tried, he couldn't stop the words. "Well, I'm pretty sure I love you, so I needed for you to have—"

Clover found himself on his back with a good three hundred and twenty-five pounds pinning him in place.

Saint's eyes glowed in a way Saint had never seen before. "Did you just tell me you love me?"

Damn. He had, and apparently, it was the wrong move. Clover knew he was being dumb. It was way too soon, except he couldn't help how he felt. Saint had slipped beneath his skin faster and harder than anyone had done before. They just felt like a miracle. He couldn't make himself take it back. Clover cleared his throat. His gaze slid away from Saint's intensity. He couldn't watch Saint reject him. "It seems so, but don't worry. I won't say it again. I know it's crazy and you're not ready to hear all that. Everything about us has been—"

Saint kissed him, cutting off the babbling before it started. Once he had Clover's attention, Saint held his stare. "Don't you dare start backtracking now. I've been sitting on those words all day, but it seems you're braver than I am. Yeah. This is something different, like you were purposely set in my path. I love you. It doesn't seem possible. I definitely can't explain it, but you're mine. It's like you were always meant to be mine."

A tear slipped from the corner of Clover's eye and slid back into his hair. "You're the greatest thing that's ever happened to me. I can't stop begging the universe for this to be real."

"It is. I know it is." Saint kissed him with all the love and longing Clover always carried in his chest. That was the kicker. Since that very first time their lips touched, Clover had known he would never go back to that one-bedroom apartment where he had suffered so much pain. Saint was his home.

That was the last coherent thought he had once Saint rocked against him. He made love to Clover. It was sweet and so fucking hot. The friction between their bodies increased as their kisses turned more passionate and hungrier. It didn't take long for that familiar pressure to addle his brain. Everything was focused on what Saint did to his cock. When an orgasm ripped through him, it hit him how real this relationship was. It was so fucking flawless, and all Clover had ever wanted. He wouldn't stop until Saint married him. Nothing less would do.

CHAPTER SEVEN

SAINT WAS FUCKING EXHAUSTED as he dragged their luggage through the door. The cabin was dark except for the Christmas lights. He had sworn he had unplugged them before they left. Since Clover had moved into his mind and set up shop, Saint hadn't thought straight. A very familiar sound cut through the dark. It had Saint dropping the luggage and tucking Clover behind his back with one arm while the other hand flipped on the lights.

"Oh. You're home."

From his back, lounging on Saint's couch, Jacobe looked totally relaxed with a gun ready to fire pointed at them.

"You've really stepped things up a notch," Saint said as dryly as possible. "Now you've decided you're ready to go to prison instead of just leaving Clover alone."

Jacobe's expression changed, turning evil and angry in a way Saint had never seen. That was saying a lot. "There's no such thing as living without Clover." The way his face and anger stayed totally focused on Saint meant Saint's large body kept Clover totally hidden from sight. Or Jacobe saw Saint as the only thing standing between him and the center of his obsession. Jacobe's rage kept him talking while Saint pulled his cellphone from his back pocket and handed it to Clover on the sly. "You don't understand! But if I let you live, you'll see. You'll see how he lights up every corner of your life and then rips it away, leaving you drowning in the dark. He won't stay with you. I mean, a boss sleeping with his employee. How cliche can you get? Don't worry, though. I'll put you out of your misery so you never have to feel this way."

Saint searched for a way to keep Jacobe talking while Clover got them help. "How long were you two together? It must've been a long time to break you like this." Saint knew the only thing Jacobe mourned was the control. He just needed Jacobe to stay focused on their conversation.

"Two years, three months, and three days. Three hundred and nighty-eight days." He took on a dreamy expression and a new horror rose inside Saint. This guy was for real insane. He wasn't just mean and controlling. The guy had lost his mind. "He smells so good, and his skin is so soft. I couldn't let him near anyone else. He's irresistible. Well, you know that. He's like staring into the face of love and knowing it's all yours."

Saint wondered if the "it" in that sentence was the love or Clover. It wasn't too much of a stretch. Jacobe obviously didn't consider Clover as a real whole person who existed without him.

"Don't worry. I'll set you free before you end up like me when Clover comes home to me."

Before Saint even had time to react, Clover stepped around him. His anger carried him across the room in a clipped pace. "For fuck's sake, Jacobe. You're being fucking ridiculous."

Saint's mouth fell open as Clover plucked the gun from his hand like a ninja. His anger obviously outweighed Jacobe's insanity. He racked the weapon, releasing the unfired shell before waving the butt at Jacobe in obvious frustration. "This is too goddamn far. Why do you think we're over? Save your breath. It's for ridiculous shit like this. Not that you have any chance of me ever taking you back, but did you really think breaking into Saint's cabin and threatening to kill—"

"Our cabin," Saint said, correcting him.

Clover didn't miss a beat. "Our cabin, threatening to kill people, would actually get me back? Murder is a damn long prison sentence. Not that any of that matters to you. I'm done with you. I've been finished with you for almost nine months and a whole year before I got brave enough to leave, and that's no one's fault but yours. Saint didn't steal me. He didn't seduce me away. We didn't even know each other back then. When will you take responsibility for your actions? You lost me. No one else. You."

Damn, he was sexy with his eyes flashing with fury. Saint was turned on and he couldn't help it.

Clover didn't let up on the berating. "Did you really think that tagging me, controlling me, hitting me, and fucking cheating on me was shit that endeared me to stay? You were an awful boyfriend. You're a terrible person. A waste of oxygen. If you think you deserve me, you're as insane as you're acting."

One of his security teams burst in, armed to the teeth and wearing Kevlar. They all froze as Clover handed Diesel the gun and walked straight into Saint's arms. For all his fury, he shook hard enough to chip a tooth. "Thank God. I was running out of things to say."

Even though he was obviously terrified and had handled the situation like a boss, Saint couldn't hold his tongue. "What were you thinking? He could've killed you."

Saint felt Clover shrug. "He could've killed me a million times over the years. But he's obviously high as a fucking kite. That always renders him useless."

He kissed Clover's temple. "You're the bravest and strongest person I know. You also looked hot as hell, berating someone. I mean, you scared the shit out of me when you stormed between that gun and me. Please don't do that again, but I was definitely turned on by your fire."

Clover chuckled. His shaking eased a hair. "Best you know what you're in for now."

"I look forward to every second."

Clover laughed again. "Good, since you're stuck with me."

"Thank God."

He loved the way Clover felt when he laughed, and the conversation was obviously easing his nerves. Saint barely noticed the police pouring in. His arms wouldn't unlock from Clover. Clover was all that mattered

"Mr. Zhao."

Clover lifted his head and looked toward the young, brown-haired cop. "It's Knack, but you can call me Clover."

At his statement, Jacobe shot to his feet and had to be restrained. He went wild, fighting against his handcuffs and the two cops holding him. "I'll fucking kill you, you motherfucker. There's no goddamn way he married you. You piece of shit. I should've just pulled the trigger when you walked through the door."

"So much for him being useless high."

Thankfully, Clover had already walked away with the officer and didn't hear his muttered words.

Saint's gaze landed on Diesel. He moved his way. They shook hands. "Thank you again for coming to the rescue. This is getting to be an all-too-common experience."

Diesel glanced toward a still struggling Jacobe, who still screamed about how Clover would only get married over his dead body. Diesel shook his head as they dragged him out the door.

"Hopefully, this'll be the last of all this."

Saint nodded. "He needs mental help. You should've heard the shit he was saying before Clover jumped his ass."

Diesel laughed. "Clover is great. You're a lucky man. If you hadn't immediately staked your claim, I might've thrown my hat in the ring." Before Saint had time to feel one way or the other, since Diesel looked like a goddamn supermodel, Diesel kept going. "Congratulations, by the way. I had to leave after the party to get home by Christmas. I love this job, but seeing my mom comes first, you know? But I heard Steel and the guys really came together to create the perfect Christmas Day wedding."

Saint couldn't stop smiling. "It was pretty perfect."

Diesel shook his head. "I'd like to say I can't believe this happened so fast, but damn. I've seen you two together. You've definitely shown there are soulmates out there."

Clover appeared at his side and hugged Saint's arm. His gaze stayed on Diesel. "Thank you so much for showing up. I was running out of steam. There's no telling what he might've done."

Diesel dipped his chin, acknowledging the appreciation. "It's all good. We'll always come when you call. Plus, this gives me the chance to switch vehicles. I came here in the SUV. I'll take the Ram back to the warehouse."

"Mr. Knack."

Saint and Clover looked over at the officer.

The guy looked at the paper he held. "Saint."

Saint kissed Clover's forehead and stepped away to answer any questions the police had. Anything to move this along so Clover and he could get back to their peaceful existence. They were still newlyweds, after all. They deserved to be alone.

In his fuzzy pjs, Clover sat curled up in Saint's lap while Saint kissed his neck. Saint's thumb swept back and forth across Clover's wedding ring. It was like he was savoring this crazy thing they had done. As much as Clover still couldn't believe he agreed, he had lost more for less in his life. He wasn't scared to take a chance. Saint was a miracle. Their wedding had been gorgeous. Thankfully, the Steel company seemed to have more than just security working for the company. Somehow, they had gotten copies of Saint's and his birth certificates and even had a judge to marry them. The guy had looked happy to do it too. It was the wildest experience of his life. Clover didn't regret a damn thing.

"I can't stop picturing you storming your way to Jacobe and snatching that gun. You nearly gave me a heart attack before immediately turning me on. Damn. You're so strong."

Clover had to clear one thing up. "I'm not strong. You forget I spent years under his thumb." Clover shrugged. "I guess him threatening to harm you was the breaking point for me. You're my person, and he wanted to rip that away from me. It wasn't happening. But I turned you on, huh? Is that why you're hard?"

The sexy chuckle Clover couldn't resist vibrated against his neck. "I'm always hard around you." His hand swept up Clover's inner thigh. He made it impossible to hang on to a coherent thought.

"Fuck." The curse came out so breathless, Clover was almost embarrassed. Almost, but he loved it. "I can't tell you how happy I am that this is us for the rest of our lives. As much as I keep trying to dredge up a single ounce of shame over how quickly things moved, I can't. I've never been so attached and certain in my life."

Saint slowly slid the zipper down on Clover's pajamas. His hand slipped inside and massaged Clover's erection. "I love you and I know you love me. Nothing else matters."

Clover let out a pant. "Damn right I love you."

Saint shot to his feet, keeping a tight hold on Clover. He turned and gently set Clover where he had been sitting. The next thing Clover knew, Saint was on his knees with Clover's cock in his mouth.

Clover ran his fingers through Saint's hair as his hips left the couch. "Goddamn, Saint. That feels good."

Saint chuckled around his erection.

The sensation had Clover writhing. He wanted to fuck Saint's mouth, but he equally wanted the blow job to last forever. Clover's gaze locked on their lit Christmas tree. They had definitely found a way to change Christmas into the happiest day of the year. On the edge of orgasm and with love driving his heart and soul, Clover had never had a clearer mind. From the moment he set eyes on Saint, there had been a spark. No way could he have known that spark was the feeling of meeting his soulmate. Apparently, fate had gotten tired of Clover fucking up and not seeing his true path. Jacobe stalking him straight into Saint's arms was the biggest gift of his entire life. A true holiday miracle.

Check out the first book in the Steel Security series, *Finding Shelter*

About the Author

CHARITY PARKERSON IS AN award-winning and multi-published author with several companies. Born with no filter from her brain to her mouth, she decided to take this odd quirk and insert it in her characters. One of her greatest loves is writing morally gray characters. You'll find them scattered throughout her hundreds of titles.

*Nine-time Readers' Favorite Award Winner

*2015 Passionate Plume Award Finalist

*2013 Reviewers' Choice Award Winner

*2012 ARRA Finalist for Favorite Paranormal Romance

*Five-time winner of The Mistress of the Darkpath

Connect with her online:

*Sign up for her newsletter: https://bit.ly/charityparkersonnewsletter

*Join her readers' group on Facebook: http://bit.ly/CharitysTribe

*Website: https://www.charityparkerson.com

*A list of her social media accounts and giveaways all in one place: http://hy.page/charityparkerson

www.ingramcontent.com/pod-product-compliance
Lightning Source LLC
Chambersburg PA
CBHW052004220626
47052CB00004B/1081